AUGENESIS

A SHORT SCIENCE FICTION STORY

SUPER GREAT CHALLENGE STORIES
BOOK 7

RYAN M. WILLIAMS

Printed in the United States of America

Glittering Throng Press

PO BOX 179

RAINIER WA 98576-0179

eBook ISBN-13: 978-1-946440-90-7

Paperback ISBN-13: 978-1-946440-91-4

GTP NO. 49
SGC NO. 07

ACKNOWLEDGMENTS

This story is one of 52 weekly stories written (and published) over a year. It's part of the Super Great Challenge (SGC) run by Dean Wesley Smith and Kristine Kathryn Rusch through the WMG Publishing workshops on Teachable. Without that challenge, this story (and the others) likely wouldn't exist.

Additionally, in creating the cover art for the stories in the SGC, I've typically used Blender—my **favorite application ever**—an open source, free, 3D modeling, digital painting, animation, sculpting, and video editing application. I've taken courses and watched tutorials from creators like Ducky 3D, Southern-Shotty, Grant Abbitt, Curtis Holt, the Blender Studio, CG Cookie, CG Boost, the Blender Guru and so many others. It's a wonderful and inspiring community.

And I'm so grateful for the **support of my members** on my site (ryan mwilliams.com) for their encouragement for this challenge. My family has also been instrumental in making this possible. It helps immensely having people behind me on this journey. Thank you.

———

CHAPTER 1

"We're going to rust."

The words fell like snowflakes in the cold air. Corner Bracket—C.B. for short—bumped over an exposed slab of concrete erupting from the ground like a broken tombstone. The fog glowed as beams from C.B.'s blue and red lights were diffused. Crispy dry leaves made soft whispers as they tumbled in the chilly breeze. C.B.'s upper section rotated, the dark lens cluster focusing on Kiera. "Did you hear me?"

At twenty-seven, Kiera had listened to C.B.'s complaints her entire life. She consulted the holographic map projected from her watch. "It isn't far. You're water-proof, and people don't rust."

C.B. made a squeaky noise of derision. "With all that iron in your blood? Don't count on it. You're rusting from the inside out."

A fallen Douglas fir crossed the broken path. Trees on the other side of it held up the end, leaving it at a thirty-degree angle. Broken and splintered branches looked like shattered legs where it had hit. Looking left, the moonlight showed the jagged remains of the stump. It'd snapped off. Maybe last winter, during the hard freeze. A whole bunch of trees had come down with the freezing rain forming ice on everything, the temperature dropping, and then the wind. With their flexibility sapped by the cold, the trees had shattered. Kiera laid a hand against the trunk, touching the rough bark, before she ducked beneath it.

A scraping noise followed, then C.B. said, "Oh swell, that's going to leave a mark."

Ferns, dogwood, and black berry vines crowded in on the path through the young wood. Enough of a gap remained between the trees leaning in from each side to allow moonlight to penetrate. Between the fog and the thicker growth on each side, the woods looked dark. Quiet, though, the sound muffled by the clinging fog. Now and then there came the sound of a bird or other small animal moving through the brush. They were the loudest things out here tonight. *Well, C.B. at least.*

The bot was a squat cylindrical shape with four articulated legs that could—when needed—carry it along at a good pace. "C.B."—Common Bot model three—aka Corner Bracket, had been her father's creation. It was designed to help out around their isolated homestead. A versatile bot to help out with chores. Fetch, carry, and haul, that was the intent. Dad hadn't anticipated that his daughter would bond with the bot, forming a life-long friendship. It didn't matter to her that C.B. was a bot created and programmed by her Dad. She didn't believe him when he told her that C.B. wasn't self-aware.

"I built it, programmed it," he had said. "You'd think I'd know if it was a person."

"I guess you're not as smart as you think," seven-year-old Kiera said.

Dad laughed and lifted his hands in defeat. "I guess not. You two be careful if you go out in the woods. Don't go past the bridge."

"We won't!"

A squawk from C.B. brought her back to the present. The bot squatted on the path in front of her, lights glowing in the fog, the lense cluster moving back and forth as it scanned the woods on each side.

"Can we go back now? It's cold and damp. Your fragile immune system shouldn't be put at risk."

Kiera extended her arm and touched the screen on her watch to project the holo of the old map she'd found. She pointed past the blinking dots that represented her and C.B.. "That's the bridge. But look, on this map there are several buildings not more than a kilometer past. I want to know why Dad always told us not to go past the bridge."

"Probably because he knew it was dangerous," C.B. said. "He protected us. We should go back."

"He protected us? He kept us in the dark, C.B.. He didn't tell us what was out here. That's not keeping us safe. He's gone now. We have to look after ourselves."

"Sure, right. By immediately going

to the place he forbid us to go. Makes sense. Nothing could go wrong with that plan."

Kiera crossed her arms. She'd dressed for the weather. Thick brown trousers, her comfortable black hiking boots, red-black flannel shirt (*one of Dad's*), and her coat of many pockets. She also had her floppy, wide-brimmed hat and a backpack with a first aid kit, flares, waterproof matches, packets of food and water, and two spare cells for C.B.—it was more than enough for the short distance they had to go. She wasn't reckless, but she had to see what was out here. Dad had never told them, and now it was too late.

She wiped fog moisture from her face and cleared her throat. "You can go back if you want. You know the way. I can't. I need to see what is out there."

Without waiting for an answer, Kiera strode off down the trail.

For a couple seconds C.B. didn't move. Just as she was starting to think it might actually go back (*except it wouldn't, would it?*), she heard it muttering to itself.

"There could be dire wolves. Or worse."

Kiera smiled to herself as she heard

its legs whine into motion and begin thumping after her, sometimes striking the concrete buried beneath the forest floor with a louder hammer strike.

CHAPTER 2

A hooting call sounded through the open concrete windows from somewhere below. Gevyn's nanonic cluster cells whispered in his thoughts. *Barred Owl, indigenous nocturnal bird.* More facts waited like shadows, if he wanted to shine the light on them. He didn't. As long as the animal left him alone, he wasn't worried about it. The data point might prove of interest when he got back—everything he gathered would get studied and analyzed, tearing into every detail to understand the ecological changes that had taken place over the past century. He was surprised to even find large structures like these still standing after all that time. Even though vegetation was doing its best to break them apart, the structures remained visible from the air.

He'd circled the site, identifying a cluster of a half-dozen large structures. This was the largest—a concrete and steel structure that still stood taller than the tall firs and other trees surrounding it. Smaller trees grew from the open windows and the flat roof.

He was glad of the protections of his environsuit and helmet. It was a cold night out there, but he was safely protected from any of the environmental hazards he might encounter. The suit was a standard nanonic, adaptive environmental unit. Flexible, tough, and equipped with enough power cells to keep him going for more than a week (*local time*) on the surface. The processors back on the scout ship could ingest local resources to safely replenish his stores, allowing him to function for an indefinite period on the surface—not that he'd be here that long.

He walked carefully across the vegetation-littered floor toward the large empty window where moonlight poured into the structure. His overlays enhanced his view, making the empty space visible. His environsuit sensors measured the floor's response to each step, radiating lines spreading out in his overlays to highlight the weaker sections of concrete. Most of it remained sound, but the environsuit systems had identified fractures and weaker sections. Give it another couple decades and the whole interior floors would probably collapse down into the basement levels. The walls (*partially or entirely*) might remain for a time, but with the loss of the floors they'd begin flexing. It wouldn't take much longer after the floor collapse before the entire building was rubble. It'd get buried by the growing forest beneath subsequent layers of decaying matter until nothing remained except a mound of rich earth entombing the rubble. In time, even the rubble beneath the earth would break down until there wasn't anything remaining.

Not while I'm here. Gevyn reached the window and put a hand on the edge to brace himself as he put one foot up on the lip and looked out at the surround forest. Beneath him a fog enshrouded the lower levels of the trees, hiding the forest floor from view. Moonlight glowed brightly against the fog. The trees stood out, details visible even without overlay enhancements. The owl noises repeated in the night. It sent a shiver down his spine, a feeling of something *alien*, like facing a xeno, which made no sense because this was *Earth*, not some xenotic planet. But Earth had its own unknown lifeforms. Earth held its dangers, no mistake. It wasn't uninhabited. They'd known that, of course. It was one fact that made the whole mission dangerous. *More dangerous*. The satellite scans showed settlements, towns, but no large-scale industrial activity. No evidence of any large ocean-going vessels or air travel. His sector maps showed a small cluster of domes and fields not far to the northeast from this location. He'd landed here to scout the ruins, rest, and then, in the early morning hours, set off to see what he could of the domes. That was an anomalous site. It suggested a technological level inconsistent with the rest of their observations.

The night appeared peaceful. Gevyn didn't trust it. The barred owl (*after he accessed a render*) looked fierce—if you were the size of a mouse or rat. Not something that he needed to worry about. He couldn't be sure, though, what else might be out there in the night. After the augenesis extinction event it was hard to know *what* he might find on this mission. Even that owl—the call sounded the same—but it might have changed more than he imagined. The augenesis put species on the same footing with bacteria and viruses, giving them easy DNA-transfer, and accelerated evolution. He'd studied the reports from the previous missions. The inhabitants of those settlements and towns scattered around the planet—some of them looked more like xenos than anything else. Augenesis had changed the planet and led to one of the worst mass extinctions in the planetary history. Those not on Earth had been spared, the planetary quarantine and blockade implemented. So terrifying was augenesis, that anyone in Sol's other in-system colonies were also quarantined until exhaustive studies showed that augenesis hadn't spread beyond Earth's biosphere. It'd been contained in time.

He turned from the window and began picking his way back along the safe paths across the floor. This building was a shell. Probably picked clean by scavengers back at the start of the augenesis. If so, the other buildings probably hadn't fared any better.

You could return, whispered the *Okanogan* in his nanonic cluster of receptor cells. *No unnecessary risks, remember?*

"It's not unnecessary," Gevyn said. "It's the point of this whole exercise, remember? Besides, if I come back, I have to spend a day in the quarantine section. We'd loose too much time."

The silence from *Okanogan* was enough of an answer.

CHAPTER 3

The bridge emerged from the fog like a ship coming to dock. Tall steel struts rose up in the gap between taller trees that stood like dark towers on each side of the river. Kiera pressed forward past several young saplings in the path (*apple trees, it looked like, probably from the taller tree beside the path*). Warty clusters of anomalous cells grew on the thin silver branches. It could be internal mutations or something created by an infection. She was careful not to disturb them, just in case. The rushing energy of the river drew her closer to the bridge. Here the ground cover thinned, the path widening and rising, pitted concrete rising into view. A brisk breeze blew along the river channel through the woods. It kept the concrete and the bridge mostly clear of dirt accumulation. It only left a few small patches where small plants fought for footing. She came to a stop when she stepped onto the bare concrete and looked up. at the structure of the bridge.

The large steel struts welded and riveted together, formed two angular arcs across the river, mirrored on the other side. At one time the steel must have been painted and protected against weathering, but no more. It was pitted and covered in rust. Visible cracks ran across the concrete deck like the lines that had formed on Papa's face and hands in the years before—

"Yes, a brilliant idea. That looks very safe," C.B. said, stopping beside her with two clanging hammer strikes of its feet against the concrete the sound echoed out along the river channel.

Kiera hadn't been here for five years. She'd made this hike with C.B. once before, coming out to *see* the bridge that she'd been forbidden to cross her entire life. It'd been bright that day, summer, when the dry heat made her feel like she could stay in the domes all day—if there hadn't been work to do. Papa had been holed up in his workshop, so after chores, she'd come out here to see it for herself. The rusted hulking structure had looked like the skeleton of a giant robot, she thought, that had fallen across the river and died. They hadn't ventured even this close before turning to flee back home.

Not this time.

C.B. extended an arm to point at the structure. "Many of the support beams have been removed."

"What?" Kiera looked again at the bridge, not sure what it meant. Then she saw it.

The metal arcs looked mostly empty. Gaps revealed in the moonlight. Here and there, though, beams remained like braces. She'd learned enough from Papa to recognize that what remained were only a few of the beams that should be holding up those arcs of metal. It explained why the concrete deck had ripples to the structure as sections had sagged beneath their own weight, the support arcs weakened by the removal of the beams.

"Did Papa do that?"

"He scavenged metal where he could. If he took metal from this bridge, it was before he made me. It seems likely."

Kiera looked down at C.B., reaching

out to touch his rounded 'head'. The bot side-stepped the contact.

"Maybe you're made—in part—from metal he scavenged from this bridge."

"Maybe you're made from parts of animals and plants you consume. What's your point?"

Kiera inhaled through her nose, smelling the damp and rich odor of the forest and the water flowing beneath the bridge. It was several meters wide. Large rectangular concrete footings supported it from beneath on each side of the river in pairs, with a third pair standing in the river itself. Each of the metal arcs came down to the point above that center support. It was dark beneath the bridge. Fog hung above the rushing water. It swirled just beneath the bridge, stirred by the breeze.

Gravel and chips of concrete ground beneath her boots as she stepped onto the broken slabs leading to the bridge. C.B. beeped sharply.

"What are you doing? That bridge is clearly structurally unsound."

"Sure it is. But I weigh hardly anything compared to the weight it is already bearing. And I walk softly. I don't think it's suddenly going to collapse if I step on it."

"Maybe not, but now you've jinxed it."

Kiera twisted around, looking down at the bot's familiar rounded head. It showed plenty of signs of wear itself. Scratches and dents on its outer casing. Damage that was—*she had to admit to herself*—her fault. She led them everywhere in the woods, up and down ravines, into risks that C.B. would never take on its own.

"Stay here," she said. "You're heavier. And your feet pounding on the concrete *might* be enough to destabilize it."

C.B. bleeped, screeched, and whistled. It rose higher on its legs, rocking forward to bring its lens cluster closer to looking her in the eyes. "No, Kiera. Don't do this. Your father wouldn't want you to risk it."

She stiffened. "Probably not, but he's gone, C.B., and what? Should I stay in the domes the rest of my life? How long will that be, alone?"

"I'll be there."

"Yes, but we need trade, C.B., Papa must have scavenged this way. There could be more that we can use on the other side of the bridge."

"He didn't go this way for trade. He

took the Cluster path out, then went South."

Kiera nodded. "I know, C.B.—he told me. Twenty kilometers to the nearest settlement. He wouldn't let me go, told me about the dangers. But now we have to look out for ourselves."

C.B.'s legs flexed, shaking the entire body from side to side. "Not this way. It's dangerous. Don't go."

"Stay here. I'll be careful. If the structure looks too unstable, I'll come back."

C.B. sagged in place until its base nearly touched the ground. "If it collapses with you, I'm throwing myself in the river."

"C.B.! Why would you say that?"

C.B. made a mournful tone. "No point continuing without you."

She *wanted* to wrap her arms around the bot and give it a hug, the way she'd done as a girl, but C.B. never understood the gesture. It avoided physical contact whenever possible.

"I'll be careful," she said, knowing also that C.B. wasn't above trying to manipulate her emotions. "Wait here."

The bot's lights dimmed and pulsed slowly, but it didn't say anything else.

Fine. C.B. could sulk. She wasn't being reckless. If Papa had scavenged metal from the bridge, he probably thought it was dangerous. Yet it still stood here, spanning the river, the moon glow against the fog showing the dark structure in contrast.

For all her arguments, her gut tightened with each step up onto the beginning of the bridge. The rusted metal structure grew larger on each side like massive arms reaching out to embrace her. The sound of the river beneath the fog was more than the roaring noise of water rushing over boulders below—the surface beneath her feet vibrated with the force of the water. It had rained these past few weeks. All that water, streams coming down the mountains and gathering in the river, it must be high in its bed right now. It was just as well that the night and fog hid the drop from view. She could sense the depth beneath her, but she couldn't see it.

Stepping onto the bridge itself, she held her breath for a couple seconds, irrationally expecting it to react somehow. Groan beneath her. Shake. Something. Nothing changed about the bridge.

Here, closer now, she saw the surface was much worse than she'd thought when she first looked at it. The upper layers of concrete were flaked and eroded away. It left the bridge with a pitted, uneven surface. Dirt and small plants clung to the roughened surface. That included large patches of green and purple moss, colors muted in the moonlight. In fact, looking at the patches and the pitting, it looked like the moss concentrated in the lower pits. *Collecting moisture?* It might also produce some sort of acid to eat away at the structure, deepening the pits, making it better at collecting moisture and protecting the moss from the sun's harsh rays during the day.

Speculation. She couldn't be sure of the moss's properties without studying samples. And she wasn't going to test her hypothesis by walking where the moss might have weakened the structure.

A low querying beep sounded behind her, from C.B..

"I'm going," she said. "Being careful, like I said."

C.B. responded with a dissatisfied burst of noise.

Ignoring the bot, Kiera took careful steps forward, sticking to the brighter bare spots of concrete where the moonlight showed it was clear. Even so, the concrete was spiderwebbed with cracks. She tested each step before taking it, pushing with the toe of her boot for any suggestion that the concrete might give away beneath her. She ignored the dark frames of metal rising on each side of the bridge. All of her attention had to be on the bridge surface, finding a safe path across.

A meter out and she could tell the surface had sagged downward. The cracks were fine dark lines. Some with thin traces of plants sticking through the wider cracks. Despite the wear, the bridge remained convincingly solid beneath her boots. She didn't relax. The part nearest the start of the bridge was above the piling below. It would be a stronger part of the bridge. The farther out she got between the two pilings, the structure would weaken.

That didn't mean it was going to collapse. The bridge stood here for decades, longer, since long before things changed, and even before she was born. It didn't seem likely that it would collapse simply because she walked on it. Animals must use the bridge to cross from one side of the river to the other. Without the bridge they would either need to fly, be able to swim a strong river, or travel up or down stream to an easier place to cross.

It was a *long* ways down to the river she could feel vibrating through the concrete beneath her feet.

A low warble from C.B. almost made her look back. She resisted. It was its worried noise. She'd asked Papa about the beeps, whistles, and other tones that C.B. made, *why did it make those noises when it could talk perfectly well?* Papa grinned, his broad face smiling, kindly dark eyes twinkling and somehow looking off into the distance. *A fancy, that's all. Something from my childhood. Bots then—fictional mind you, in movies—made noises like that. You don't like it?* She had assured him it was fine. She'd only been curious. She didn't understand about movies, not really, he had tried to explain and she knew it was like stories and understood fictional. Made up stories. Pretend. She knew all about that. She played games with C.B. that were fictional.

Now she understood that C.B. made those noises to express its emotions. It worried about her (*whether Papa had believed it or not*). In a real sense, they were siblings, she and C.B., both Papa's creations. Mama had helped too, before she died.

Shaking her head as if that could clear the memories like cobwebs, Kiera focused on the cool night, the rolling fog beneath the bridge with tendrils reaching up the sides like tentacles, and the cracked and warped concrete beneath her feet. The bridge looked unstable. For all of her confidence that it could stand her weight, she couldn't be entirely sure that was true. It was also aways possible that she had spectacularly bad timing to try crossing the bridge now—if this was when it finally collapsed.

She kept to the outer edge of the bridge, near the dark rusted metal structure, figuring if the bridge collapsed it would do so where the deeper sections sagged.

A short distance on, carefully testing each step, she saw movement on the bridge's surface away to her right. Not more than a meter away. She froze and looked carefully, trying to spot what had moved.

It was fog swirling beneath the bridge. She was looking *through* the bridge. Not with an unexpected talent—there was a large crumpled hole in the deck. Fragments of concrete clung around the lip, encrusted with the moss, hanging from rusted metal bars. It was one of the pitted areas. It looked like the moss had eaten through enough to cause the concrete to break and fall away. Larger cracks traced in the moss, radiated out from the hole. The gap was large. It spanned nearly half the bridge's width like a wide rough slash in the surface.

Kiera prodded at the concrete ahead with her foot. The cracks from the hole came within a dozen centimeters of the edge of the bridge. Long tendrils of moss poked up out of the cracks like grass. She added more weight to her foot, ready to jump back if she felt the concrete shift.

It didn't move. It was solid under foot despite the disturbing webbing of cracks. She gritted her teeth and put all of her weight forward. The concrete held. She exhaled and carefully stepped onto the next section between the cracks, testing, prodding, gradually adding weight. Without the moonlight she wouldn't have been able to see the cracks. She completed the step and searched the surface ahead for the next spot to step. More cracks traced a network of lines across the concrete ahead. Moss pushing up between the cracks, dark purple with green tips, colors barely visible.

Kiera hesitated, studying the surface. The hole was long, but narrow, with fragments hanging from the rusted metal. It reminded her of a mouth full of rotten teeth. Teeth fuzzed over with the moss that had weakened the structure. It was a low point in one of the ripples in the surface. It *looked* almost like something had fallen to the bridge, breaking through in a weakened section. Looking up, her eyes traced the dark lines of the rusted girders above. One of the cross beams between the arches was missing. Looking at the remaining one above this section, she could easily imagine it breaking free, falling, shattering the concrete deck when it struck. Punching a hole through the bridge where the moss and water had already weakened the structure.

The damage might be worse than she could see. The cracks ahead radiated out from the end of the ragged tear. Her weight might not be enough to cause the entire bridge to collapse—but this part? *Maybe.* The section ahead wasn't wide but there was nowhere to step that was free of the cracks. The smart thing, the *safe* thing, would be to turn back now. She could try going around to the other side of the hole. She might find the other side was less damaged than this. Except it was such a narrow band ahead that was badly cracked, less than a meter. Past that point, the concrete looked solid enough, rising as it neared the bridges' mid-point.

And if she turned back now and tried to find a different way around, C.B. would get more frantic. She didn't want to risk having the robot coming out here in some sort of bid to save her.

Taking a deep breath, she shifted her weight and probed forward with her left foot, closer to the edge of the bridge. Not too close. She didn't want to look down at the fog illuminated by moonlight. Just enough to try and minimize her weight on the cracks.

She shifted weight forward and the concrete held. She moved her weight onto that foot and the concrete remained steady even with cracks that ran—*literally*—beneath her foot.

Breathing a bit easier, she reached her right foot forward to test another spot. Cracked, but they looked like hairline cracks. She shifted more weight forward, easing into it.

A low crack sounded, splitting the quiet, and the segment beneath her right foot shifted slightly.

Kiera froze in place. *Slowly.* She eased her right foot back up.

A sound like the groan of a sleeping haunt came from the concrete beneath her. The surface beneath her left foot tilted fractionally beneath her. Gut taunt, Kiera shifted some of her weight forward again, balancing it between the two unstable points like she was walking a tight-rope.

Rope. She should have brought *rope.*

Another thought followed immediately. *C.B. was going to gloat about being right when she got out of this.*

As soon as she figured out how. Then she'd be happy to hear it gloat.

CHAPTER 4

ensitive mics picked up and amplified the sounds on the ground floor before Gevyn reached it. He stopped on the stairwell he'd used to gain access to the upper floors of the structure and listened. It was footsteps, clearly. It sounded like someone walking around the lower level. That was potentially alarming, he had no intention of making contact with any of the formerly human inhabitants. Worse, though, was the *snuffling* sounds. Wet, snorting, sniffing and snuffling sounds (*amplified by his suit*) came from below. Whatever was down there, it might be scenting him. Even tracking him.

Launching drones, said *Okanogan's* voice in his head. *Stay where you are.*

Gevyn drew his blaster. It held a

hundred mag-fired plasma rounds in each clip. Even one shot should be sufficient to bring down a large predator.

Or bring down the structure on your head.

"I'm not going to shoot unless I have to," Gevyn said silently, using his nanonic connection with the scout ship.

Several windows opened up, one column to his left and right, four squares stacked, in his overlays. The views from the drones. He watched the feed as the drones flew a fast pattern around the structure. They flew silently with no lights, relying on spectrum enhancement to make the area as bright as daylight. They closed in from all sides around the building, dropping lower to the ground as they neared, preparing to enter through the openings in the sides. As they closed in the drones identified a figure standing in the structure's ground floor.

"Damn, that's big," Gevyn said.

Nearly three meters tall. More, if you include the antlers.

The figure—and it was a *figure,* standing on two legs, with two arms— was massive. Its limbs and trunk might have been made from trees, they were so thick. It's arms were long and extremely muscled, like the rest of it. All clearly visible since the thing had no visible hair. The skin looked thick, grey in the enhanced view from the drones. The hands looked odd. Gevyn understood when it lifted its hands, arm bending at the elbow to a ninety-degree angle. The fingers were long and tipped with dark claws, but none as dramatically as the thumb. If there was a thumb. The thick round base sprouted into a curved and serrated claw eighteen centimeters long (*according to the drone scans*). Like a bio-logical sickle, no, a *hook*. Worse than that. Those hands were designed to hook prey, the fingers closing around the victim like a spiked trap. Gevyn was pretty sure once this thing got a grip on something, it wasn't going to let go. It had the muscles and equipment to bring down large prey.

He didn't want to test his suit. He doubted it'd hold up against that crea-ture's grip.

As bad as that looked, the creature's head was even worse. It was large, sit-ting above massive neck muscles, a thick round skull topped by a massive spread of pointed antlers. Gevyn thought that it might be wearing them, a decorative crown of sorts, until he saw how the flesh of the head made rings around the antlers. It had *grown* those antlers itself. Each a meter long. The face extended forward in a long triangular muzzle. Thick lips wrinkled, showing glimpses of sharp teeth. A wet black nose flared at the end of the muzzle, sniffing the air. It's head turned to each side and he saw the eyes were large, round, and had bright blue irises. *Human-looking* eyes, surrounded by thick eyelids, beneath a solid brow ridge.

"It knows the drones are there," Gevyn said.

It doesn't know what drones are, the scout ship answered. *It can't.*

An alarmed snort was loud enough that Gevyn didn't need any enhancement to hear it. The creature bayed loudly and crouched slightly, arms spreading and rising to each side. It looked ready to spring. The head swung around, eyes narrowing as it searched for whatever it had noticed.

"It picked up on something." He lifted the blaster and pointed it down the stairwell. If it came this way, he'd take the risk of shooting and hope the structure held up.

Okanogan said, *I will attempt to use the drones to drive it away.*

"Go ahead. I don't want to shake hands with that."

It will make for a fascinating report.

"Yeah, swell. Do it."

The drones on the west side of the building turned on flashing lights and began emitting a siren noise.

The creature snarled in their direction. It swiped its claws through the air —no where near the drones themselves —in a show of defiance. It didn't retreat.

"It doesn't look like it wants to leave," Gevyn said. "This might be its den. If it is territorial, it might defend it."

It must leave before you can descend the stairs.

He didn't disagree.

I will attempt to harass it with the drones.

Those four drones flew rapidly at the figure while continuing to flash lights and blast the siren noises.

With impressive agility, the creature spun away from the drones and jumped aside. *Okanogan* wouldn't have hit it with the drones, but it couldn't know that. As the drones shot past it reached out in a blur of motion (*caught by the silent drones on the east side of the building*), caught the nearest drone in one large hand. It clenched its hand and that massive thumb claw cut right through the carbon-reinforced hull of the drone. The feed from the drone died. Then it hurled the crushed remains with terrible accuracy—hitting a second drone. Both drones blew apart from the impact.

"Shit," Gevyn said, awed, and terrified.

Fascinating. It's reactions suggest intelligence and cunning.

"Terrific. Now that you've got its attention—make the drones flee. Maybe it'll give chase."

Good idea.

The drones on the east side of the building lit up and swept inside. The tone they made shifted to a panicky sounding warble. They joined the remaining drones. All making screaming, scared sounds, they flew a quick, seemingly disorganized pattern around the room. The creature growled at them, swiping with its long arms, but *Okanogan* kept the drones out of its reach. Then all of them sped out the openings on the east side into the night, wailing like scared wil-o-wisps as they speed off into the night away from the scout ship and the ruins.

Except one. In the confusion of the others, *Okanogan* had one drone go silent and dark near the ceiling, unmoving. On its feed, Gevyn watched and heard the creatures deep, *enthusiastic* growl, then it bounded forward in pursuit of the drone swarm. The silent watcher trailed along after.

Now. Leave the structure, said the scout ship.

CHAPTER 5

The sound of metal against concrete, like a hammer blow, sounded behind Kiera. She didn't turn her head. She didn't move. "C.B., don't come on the bridge. It isn't stable."

"My weight is distributed over a wider area," C.B. said. "I can reach you."

"Or you'll tip the balance and send us both crashing down into the gorge." The fog hid the depths below, but she remembered from that past visit how the rock dropped down, not straight, but narrower at the top than bottom. Dark wet rock, with plants and moss growing on the cracks in the first few meters, then just stone below. The water far below rushed along multiple channels carved through the rock. When the water was higher, it covered all of those. Even if she could survive a fall that far (*and not get crushed by falling pieces of the bridge*) the water would sweep her under and away in its freezing embrace, pounding her against wet rock. No way to get a purchase, even if she could stay awake. Which was a fantasy, because the fall would kill her.

"Go back and get a rope," she said. "You can throw it to me and pull me back if the bridge collapses."

"It might collapse before I get back."

"Then you better hurry," she said.

"You'll remain still?"

"Yes. Please, C.B., it's the only way." Except if she felt like the surface was collapsing beneath her, and then she was going to try and jump clear. Reach one of the rusted girders where she might be able to hang on.

A low warble of distress came from the bot.

She opened her mouth to tell it to hurry again, but there came an answering wailing cry from the far side of the bridge. *What is that?*

White lights appeared flashing and moving as rapidly as birds—but no birds flew such dizzying spirals and turns—between the dark trees. Along with the lights came the electronic wailing and squeals that sounded like C.B., and sounded scared. Whatever they were, they were headed straight for the bridge.

A loud, deep-throated roar, furious and blood-chilling, burst out in the woods. She heard branches breaking. The sound of something large charging through the woods.

It's chasing them. The lights grew brighter, screaming as they fled the roaring thing behind them.

"What is it?" C.B. said.

Kiera couldn't answer. She remained frozen in place, not daring to shift her weight on the unstable concrete.

Things she couldn't make out past the bright lights, streamed out of the forest, flying overhead. They shot out over the bridge, still screaming. She clapped her hands over her ears and felt the concrete shift slightly beneath her feet. She tensed, ready to jump away.

The wailing noises the things were making cut out. They spun in a quick circle above the bridge and the lights shone down on her. Surrounded her in a bright spotlight. Kiera squinted against the light and struggled to hold her balance.

Another deep roar sounded in the woods. The light had ruined her night vision. All she could see past the lights shining on her was darkness. Branches snapped. She heard heavy footfalls. Something else was coming and these flying machines (*they had to be machines*) had lit her up like a target for whatever was chasing them.

CHAPTER 6

Halfway to the scout ship, Gevyn saw the drone feed change as they flew out of the forest. A decaying bridge structure rose out of the night over a deep gorge the survey had shown, thick fog obscuring the river beneath from view. The creature was running, still followed by the silent watching drone, continuing the chase after the remaining drones.

He skidded to a stop when he saw the lithe figure standing on the broken bridge, legs spread, not moving as the drones sped over the bridge.

"What's that?"

It looks like a young woman. She had clapped her hands over her ears. The scout ship canceled the drones' alarmed noises and circled them, shining the lights on the bridge.

It was in bad shape. What remained of the metal structure decayed and rusted. A large hole stretched partly across the bridge near the woman. The way she was standing, it looked like she was afraid of falling. Maybe she had been trying to cross the bridge and discovered it was more unstable than expected. He caught a bright flash on the drone feed and pointed at the one in question.

"Look, there, behind her at the end of the bridge."

The drone feed he'd pointed at shifted, moving and redirecting the beam of its light. It illuminated a squat cylindrical metal shape that stood on four thick legs ending in points. It had its own lights and a cluster of dark lenses that pointed back at the drone.

"A *robot*? How is there a robot?"

Okanogan's voice was calm in his nanonic cell cluster. "Apparently, there is someone still with advanced technology on Earth."

A roaring noise on the feed brought Gevyn's attention back to the other drones above the bridge. They had her highlight on the bridge—and that creature was coming. It'd be there soon in its fury to catch the invading drones.

Gevyn turned around and ran, activating muscle enhancement cells along with the suit's powered assist.

This is unadvisable. You should return.

"And leave her to that creature? No. We're going to help her."

That is contrary to our directives.

"She has a robot." He ran easily, overlays showing him the path clearly. He'd pay for using the enhancement cells later with muscle cramps and sore joints. But there wasn't time. On the drone feed, the creature had already crashed out of the woods. Seeing its prey hovering above the bridge, it threw back its head and roared—arms wide as it bayed a challenge at them. "Distract it! Keep it away from her!"

Gevyn ran on.

CHAPTER 7

When the monster crashed out of the woods, Kiera felt ice form in her veins. A couple of the machines shone lights on it, throwing it into clear relief. She shivered. Papa had warned her, hadn't he? He told her not to go past the bridge. This must be why.

She knew of things like this monster. Papa had explained augenesis to her, the history of what had happened to the planet. It was obvious that the monster had human DNA in its background, but evolved into something terrifying and predatory, that easily massed several times her own mass.

It gave a deafening roar at the machines over the bridge. It hadn't seen her yet, focused as it was on them. They were more of a mystery. She couldn't imagine where they had come from. *Flying machines*? Papa's bots worked the fields and the domes, they didn't fly. He'd told her about machines that flew in the past. *Airplanes. Helicopters. Missiles.* He showed her pictures of such things—and the terrible violence when they were used as weapons. The machines above the bridge must be something like those. They might be automated, but they might also be controlled by someone.

Papa had said that people in the settlements didn't have technology like that. No electronics. No electricity. It was one of the reasons he never let anyone come to their homestead. They had to keep their homestead a secret.

With slow, stalking steps, the monster roared again. It circled to the side. She could almost see it thinking, trying to figure if it could climb the girders fast enough to reach the flying machines. Then the massive head, with a long, pointed muzzle, and spiky antlers swung around and stopped—focused on her. No question.

Frantic warbles from C.B. behind her. "Kiera, run!"

She didn't move. If she did, this section of the bridge might collapse. She stared back through the lights from the machines at the monster. It held that position for a couple more heartbeats.

Then it charged for the bridge.

CHAPTER 8

The dark forest flowed past Gevyn like water as he ran. He had to watch where he was going, but his attention was partially on the feed from the drones. He couldn't get there in time to stop the creature—not unless *Okanogan* was able to distract it.

It saw her. Its body trembled when the head fixed on the woman.

"Distract it!"

The creature bounded forward, drones forgotten as it focused on the woman stuck out there on the bridge.

Gevyn ran as hard as he could. The drone feeds jumped into motion, drones going dark and flashing back as they dove at the creature, harassing it, avoiding the long sweeps of its arms.

CHAPTER 9

S*he was going to die.* Kiera knew it the instant the monster charged. The blood lust was clear in the massive predator. It didn't care about the machines any longer. It'd seen her, seen *prey*, and it was coming.

She held her muscles in place. C.B. was screeching behind here somewhere, but she ignored it too. All of her attention was on the thunderous beast charging toward her.

It's hairless body shone in the lights from the harassing machines, gleaming a dark reddish hue glistening with sweat. Lips had curled back from its open mouth, showing rows of sharp teeth. As it ran—a very human stride— it extended long arms that ended in clawed hands. Instead of a thumb, it had curved claws like massive meat hooks. If it caught her, those hands would be like traps, locked in her flesh while it brought its teeth in to rip and tear.

The flying machines dove and flew at it. Dark, then flashing lights in its face, a harassing swarm. It swung its arms, slashing with those claws, and missed. The flying machines twisted and flew back out of reach. They harried it, driving at it—trying (*so it seemed to her*) to turn it away from her.

The monster roared in frustration and anger. Its pace faltered as it reached the concrete surface of the bridge.

Kyla yelled at the machines, not knowing if they could understand, or if someone was controlling them. "No! Leave it!" She waved her arms. "Leave it!"

CHAPTER 10

When the woman yelled in perfectly intelligible speech, telling them to *leave it*, he couldn't believe his ears. He was nearing the edge of the forest. He'd get there soon and didn't know what he'd do when he got there.

What does she mean?

"Pull the drones back," Gevyn said, fearing what was going to happen. "Let's trust she knows what she is doing."

CHAPTER 11

As one, the swarm of machines spiraled up and circled the bridge, lights illuminating the area. As soon as they stopped harassing it, the monster's attention snapped back to her. It didn't hesitate. It roared and charged out onto the bridge with loud, pounding steps.

C.B. emitted a squeal behind her.

Kiera braced herself. She held herself ready. *It would pounce.* When it got close enough, it would pounce, intending to grab her, impale her.

Her muscles tensed. Concrete shifted slightly beneath her feet.

Far sooner than she expected, the monster leapt. The massive legs propelled that body up into the air, stretching out its arms.

Kiera threw herself forward into a

roll. Concrete made cracking sounds beneath her. She came up on her feet and sprang for the girder at the side of the bridge. She caught it, rust abrading her hands and felt the wind of something passing her head. She swung about and saw strands of her hair drifting down toward the bridge.

Past her, at the spot where she had stood, the monster crashed into the bridge surface. The weakened concrete shattered. Roaring defiance, the monster vanished into the fog with the falling concrete and broken metal. The bridge shook. Other sections cracked and sagged, tearing away to drop out of sight.

Kiera wrapped her arms around the girder and held on, hoping it wouldn't collapse.

A low thunderous noise built up as more of the bridge broke and collapsed. Metal screamed as it twisted and snapped. The entire opposite side of the bridge peeled away in sections and fell into the gorge. The noise was deafening for several seconds. It felt like the world collapsing.

Then the noise died away. Kiera remained clinging to the girder. As the last of the vibrations faded, she looked around and found herself standing on an isolated pinnacle. The girder was torn off at a joint above her. She was holding onto the stump, above the central bridge pier. Nothing connected her pinnacle to either side of the gorge. Only broken fragments stuck out over the edge of the gorge.

"Kiera!" C.B. called. "Are you okay?"

"So far," she said. "But I'm stuck."

A low distressed warble came from the bot.

Behind her, a male voice said, "May I help?"

CHAPTER 12

Gevyn stood near what remained of the bridge on this side of the river—astounded by the woman's bravery and agility. She had timed her move perfectly, rolling beneath the creature's leap, then jumping to catch that girder. Even so, he'd seen how close the swing of the creature's clawed hand had come to her head.

And then it had brought down the whole bridge with the impact of its landing.

Despite it collapsing around her, the woman hung onto the girder and didn't fall. When it was done, he heard her talking with the bot on the opposite side of the river.

"May I help?" he said.

The drones provided plenty of light.

When she turned his way, his breath caught. She was lovely. Fair, delicate features, with a pointed chin and wide, expressive, dark green eyes beneath the floppy hat she wore. The strands of hair that escaped looked dark and curly. She wore advanced textile clothing, utilitarian, with a coat that had lots of pockets and a backpack—none of it had slowed her when she made her move. Her perch was precarious. A narrow island of broken concrete with the rusted girder sticking up at an angle. It was amazing that she hadn't fallen.

"That'd be appreciated," she said, quickly recovering from her obvious surprise at seeing him there in his suit. "I forgot to pack a rope."

"I've got a better option." He sent to *Okanogan, Use the drones to make a platform for her. Bring her to this side of the river.*

Not the other side?

No.

"Hang on," he told her.

CHAPTER 13

The fact that a man was standing at the other side, wearing a technologically advanced suit, was one of the most surprising things about tonight. He sounded friendly. She didn't know why he was wearing the suit. His face through the transparent front of the helmet, lit by lights inside, was youthful with a strong jaw and pale blue eyes. She'd never seen eyes like that. Her insides were shaking. Her hands hurt where they'd been scraped by the rust.

C.B. whistled alarm.

The flying machines descended all around her, closing in and then they clicked together beside her. She couldn't tell what made it possible for them to fly. They were silent when they weren't making alarmed sounds. Each fitted into the next and in seconds there was a large circular platform waiting for her.

"I suggest you sit," the stranger said.

Not sure at all that her legs could hold her up much longer, Kiera agreed. She had to trust the stranger, though she was wary. His technology was very advanced and she didn't understand what he'd been doing here with his flying machines harassing that monster. At the moment, however, if she didn't get off this girder, she was likely to fall. Carefully, testing with her foot first and finding the platform stable, she trusted her weight to it and sank down. She sat and pulled her knees up to her chest, wrapping her arms around them.

The machines, now acting as one, carried her smoothly across the river toward the opposite side and the waiting stranger. The platform stopped when it was above solid ground. The stranger extended his hand to her and she took it, glad for the assistance as he drew her to her feet. He held her hand as she stepped down from the machines. Across the river C.B. warbled plaintively.

"Who are you?" she said. "Where do you come from?"

He was handsome, she decided, behind the helmet. He had short blonde hair. And he looked entirely human, unaffected by augenesis. Her breath caught. *The suit, it was to protect him from augenesis.*

"You're from space," she said, answering her own question. "One of the colonies?"

He seemed to think for a second, before saying, "Yes. My name is Gevyn. I'm here on a scouting mission—I'm surprised that you know about the colonies. May I ask how you know?"

"Papa taught me," she said. "I've studied all of the sciences, literature, history—he said it was important we don't forget."

"I'd like to meet him," Gevyn said. "May I ask your name?"

She flushed, embarrassed that she hadn't said. "Kiera Pope. Please to meet you. Is Gevyn your given name, or your surname?"

"Ah, given name. I'm Gevyn Light." His eyes went distant for a second. He shook his head. "Do you live in the dome structures across the river?"

"Yes," she said. She felt something stirring inside her, a flutter of excitement. *People from the colonies were back on*

Earth. Exactly what Papa had predicted. "Would you like to see them?"

He smiled at her. "I would. Very much."

She looked doubtfully at the platform the flying machines had made. "Can that carry us both?"

"Yes," Gevyn said, "but I have a better idea."

Above them a dark shape bigger than the fallen bridge appeared against the sky, outlined in blue lights. The platform split back into individual flying machines and spiraled up into the night, flying up to the —

"Is that a spaceship?"

"Yes, that *Okanogan.*"

She giggled delightedly and grabbed his arm. She turned and shouted across the river, pointing up with her free hand. "Look, C.B.! A spaceship! Like Papa said!"

From across the river came a querulous whistle.

Kiera laughed and looked up at Gevyn. He gazed back down at her and smiled. She wished he wasn't wearing that suit, because right then she really wanted to kiss him. She flushed at the thought, smiling when he said, "What?"

"Later," she said. "I want to see your ship."

———

ABOUT THE AUTHOR

Ryan M. Williams is a full-time career librarian and a multi-genre writer with over twenty books. He writes across a range of genres including science fiction, fantasy, paranormal, mystery, horror, and romance. He earned a Master of Arts degree in writing popular fiction from Seton Hill University and a Master of Library and Information Science from San Jose University. His short fiction has appeared in Pulphouse Fiction Magazine, On Spec Magazine, and anthologies from Pocket Books and WMG Publishing.

- •Killing Dead Things

FILMING DEAD THINGS

Filming the Inquisition at work made Stefan Roland's ground-breaking documentary directing career—calling him the Jane Goodall of Dead Things.

- •Farm of the Dead Things

- •Mall of the Dead Things

- •War of the Dead Things

- •Trailer Park of the Dead Things

SCIENCE FICTION STORIES & NOVELS

Discover more science fiction with these books.

- •Infestation

- •Europan Holiday

- •Stowaway to Eternity

- •Crunch Bang: The Chrystal Eagle Stories

- •Space Monkeys: A Short Science Fiction First Contact Story

- •Invasion of the Book Snatchers: A Short Science Fiction Story of Small-Town Terror

ROMANCE BY KATE N. RYAN

And if you like romance and comedy, the books by KATE N. RYAN will tickle your funny bone—and more.

- Watching You Sleep: a laugh out loud romantic comedy

- Tom Scratch: A Short Fantastic Romance Story

9 781946 440914